pure evil

BY SAMANTHA MACKENZIE

The **Magic of the Vampire** Saga
love / luck
pure / evil

For more titles, visit
SamanthaMacKenzieBooks.com

SAMANTHA MACKENZIE

pure evil

MAGIC OF THE VAMPIRE
PREQUEL NOVELETTE

Cover design by Maria Spada
mariaspada.com

Edited by Michelle Rascon
editorrascon.com

Typeset in 12/16 pt Garamond
Interior design and production management
by Samantha Brennan

This edition edited in US English

A catalogue record for this book is available
from the National Library of Australia

ISBN: 978-0-6450328-2-6 (paperback)
ISBN: 978-0-6450328-3-3 (e-book)

For my children, who always ask for stories
about the way their world began

1665

CENTRAL IRELAND

PART ONE: SLAYER

CHAPTER ONE

Cathal balanced a silver-coated knife in each hand, deftly shifting their weight as he threw one, then the other, at his imaginary enemy.

Thunk-thunk.

The pointed blades sank into their marks on the wooden wall, quivering on either side of a heart-shaped scrawl perfectly positioned inside the painted silhouette of a man.

Cathal rolled his shoulders, then paced the seven steps' distance to retrieve his weapons. Yanking out the daggers, he turned them over to inspect the blades. These knives were too fine for ordinary murder.

But then, Cathal wasn't an ordinary murderer.

On the other side of the room, Cathal's cousin, Sean, a boy—no, a man—two years older than Cathal's fourteen years, determinedly parried with his father. Each was armed with a silver-set sword, plain but made well and expertly balanced. The sharp sound of metal striking metal was jarring yet familiar, and it gave Cathal comfort. The men did this every day, and today was a day like any other.

It was.

Cathal walked to the window and feigned interest in the street outside. In truth, he was anxious to measure the color of the sky. It was pearling in the east, the sun almost ready to declare the day begun. Cathal cast his gaze down the road this way and then that. No sign of his father.

Perhaps there was still hope today *would* be like yesterday, and the day before, and the day before that.

Cathal bowed his head and mouthed a fervent prayer that his father would stay away.

The door at the rear of the house banged open, letting in first a gust of dry air and then Adam, who strode in with another big man on his heels. Adam was a strapping man, ten years Cathal's senior, and already married. His companion was his wife's brother, dependable and discreet, strong of arm, and up to the task.

Adam took quick stock of the room and made straight for Cathal. He jerked the curtains closed at the window but did not scold his younger brother for having had them open.

"Have you heard from Father?"

Cathal shook his head, relieved he had this good news to share. Adam grimaced and peeked out through a small space he'd tweaked in the curtains.

Cathal wondered if Adam would agree their father's

absence was indeed good tidings.

In a corner of the room, their young sister sat with wide eyes on the men around her, the newcomer examining a set of silver stilettos that, a moment before, had been hidden under the floorboards.

Alson believed as Cathal did. Their father's failure to appear this morning was a godsend.

Cathal looked away before his heart hurt further.

Abruptly, Adam spun and dashed to the door, reaching it the exact moment it was flung open from the outside.

And there was their father.

The tall, red-haired man hastily entered and closed the door behind him. Adam helped as he removed his overcoat.

Domnall looked deathly unwell, worse than the last time he'd returned home. His skin was wan, with a sheen of sticky sweat on his brow. His tall body was emaciated, his shoulders bent, his clothes soiled, and Cathal swallowed against the lump of grief that had jumped up to choke him.

He couldn't will his legs to move, to go to him. His knees were locked tight against the threat of buckling altogether.

Domnall fidgeted unnervingly and seemingly involuntarily. Everyone looked up from their distractions to watch him with careful gazes, but Domnall's eyes darted all about, never resting on anyone or anything for long, until they landed on Cathal. At the sight of his younger son, Domnall's face brightened a little, lucidity gleaming there for the shortest spell, and he reached out an arm. Cathal went to him reluctantly.

The man had never been the same after the succubus had found him. She had professed to love him, had declared her desire to return to her mortal existence and be with Domnall in the natural way, and yet her magic cared nothing for her intention. It continued to destroy Domnall with a single will: to steal a man's dreams, to consume a man's soul, to drain a man's blood, to end a man's life.

If the demon loved him, she would have abandoned Domnall long ago.

The old man's hand was clammy skin over sinew and bone. It was unpleasant to touch, but Cathal returned his father's desperate grip, and he thanked the heavens his mother was dead. She'd been saved from bearing witness to her husband's consorting with demons, spared the heartache and shame of her husband's corruption.

"Yes, yes," Domnall whispered, spittle flying from his lips as he nodded approvingly at what he saw around the room. "Today. It will be today."

"We are ready," Adam assured him, setting a comforting hand on his thin shoulder. Cathal saw Adam flinch at the bones beneath the fabric of Domnall's shirt, and yet, how could a son pull away from the man who sired him?

How could he turn from the man who wanted to save the world?

"Good, boys, good." Domnall absently patted at the folds of his tunic and trousers as though looking for something he'd lost, and he licked his lips nervously. "Silver knives, daggers, swords…You have them?"

"We do," Adam soothed.

"When do we leave?" Sean demanded, in a tone too eager for Cathal's comfort.

"Wait!" Cathal cried. When his father and brother locked their eyes on him, his face burned with self-consciousness, but he had spoken now and couldn't take it back, and he wanted to voice his worry. This could be his only chance. "Are we sure this is right?"

Cathal cringed as his father squeezed his hand, demonstrating a strength that belied his ailing frame.

"*She* says it is right, and *she* is sure," Domnall ranted, his eyes fevered like those of a madman. "She knows, yes, she does. She wants to save me."

"Of course, Father," Adam agreed easily. "Cathal understands that."

Domnall seemed placated, and Adam motioned for one of the other men to attend to him so he could pull Cathal away. When they'd moved to the other side of the room, Adam bent his head into Cathal's ear and pitched his voice low so nobody could hear his words.

"This is our only chance," Adam said tightly, "else he is lost to us. If this is a fool's errand or trickery or…It is of no import. We must murder the king of demons—as the succubus says, with a blade of silver to his heart—and restore sense to the world. Only then may we hope to save our father. We must try. Our lives now are hardly worth the breath in our lungs—not with vampires lying in wait every night, not with our blood at risk every moment, and our souls laid bare every time we dare sleep."

Cathal knew Adam spoke true—the vampires were many and cruel, the incubi and succubi fewer but more pitiless for it—but Cathal ached for a better way. Walking into the Master of Fear's lair was suicide, and he could not believe a simple silver dagger would save them from death.

And yet, it was a simple fact: there was no other way. Domnall's succubus and her wild claims were the first rays of light in a relentless demonic darkness. It was natural to move toward it, to crave the warmth of it on their faces.

So Cathal focused on the next step only, not the horror waiting a hundred steps ahead. He turned from Adam, unable to put his resolution into words, and spun his silver daggers over his wrists, his knuckles, the backs of his hands, before grasping the hilts and launching them again at the shadow-villain on the timber wall. They flew true and—*thunk-thunk*—hit the monster in its painted heart.

Adam clasped Cathal on the shoulder, his fingers digging in deep to express all the emotions he, too, couldn't say aloud, and together they took that first step toward the murder that needed to be done.

CHAPTER TWO

They knew where to find him. Everyone knew the Master of Fear lived in the tumbled-down castle over the hill on the northern border of the endless woods, yet nobody Cathal knew had ever seen him. It was a testament to his arrogance, or perhaps his absolute power—nay, both—that the Master walked the place night and day and turned out into the world dozens upon dozens of bloodsucking, soul-stealing demons, and no one had put an end to either him or his wicked experiments.

It was not for lack of trying.

In the beginning, more than three hundred years gone, he had been a chieftain or some such, the stories said, and it was considered an honor to attend his hedonistic parties and sacred ceremonies. Many envied those chosen to go into the castle, but soon, whispers ran like water about those who never returned—or worse, those who did and were greatly changed.

It wasn't done to question a man of such power, but within three generations, all who lived near the castle knew this lord was not of mortal making. Too many sons and daughters had been lost to his depraved ways, and a plague was upon them.

The Master was a maker of vampires—and worse.

Some braver folk had tried to kill him, of course, but all had failed. Some of those men were Turned, returning from their incursions as pale as corpses, their lips stained red with blood and their eyes as dark and empty as the depths of a dried-up well. They entered their villages and slaughtered their neighbors, then disappeared into the night.

The luckiest and most holy of the brave didn't come out of the castle at all. They went in with pure intentions and were never seen again, assumed dead.

Death was preferable to eternity as a vampire.

Yes, in the beginning, they had tried to kill the king of hell, but there was only ever defeat, and then despair. Daily prayer, a chaste heart, and locked doors after sundown were a good man's best and only lines of defense.

And then a succubus fell in love with a mortal, and she offered humanity its first hope in thirteen generations.

Her name was Isavell.

Cathal knew his father had been taken by the devil the moment Isavell spied him and chose him for her own. Cathal's mother had long passed from illness—he remembered nothing about her but the song she would hum to him at night—and Domnall had not looked at another after her death. When Isavell arrived in their village, by night, as the succubus does, and by stealth, as is the way of the vampire, she knocked on their door in the darkness, as only a demon would.

Cathal begged his father to keep the door closed to the evil most certainly waiting on the other side, but when she called for Domnall by name, in a voice so beguiling, the old man was lost to him forever. She stood there under the moon, clad in garments so worn they could not conceal the incandescence of her skin, the curve of her breast, the shape of her hip, the length of her calf. She had the face of an angel with a mouth made for sin. Isavell beckoned, and Domnall followed her into the night and out to the woods.

That night, Cathal had lain awake as he prepared the words he would need to tell his brother and sister that the succubus had seduced their father. He did not sleep—he did not dare—and when light broke over the horizon, Cathal rose and made ready to tell his family their father was dead.

Then the door opened, and Domnall entered.

His face was drawn, his eyes wide and ringed with circles as dark as bruises. His hair was mussed, his clothes caked with dirt and grass, and his hands twitched and wrung by turns.

Never mind, Cathal rejoiced. *He is alive!*

But his relief was short-lived.

Of what value is life when the succubus has your soul?

Domnall returned to her, night after night, and his body wasted as it corrupted with wickedness. Cathal said nothing about it for many a day, not wanting to admit that his father was undone, until Domnall declared that Isavell had shared the method by which they could vanquish her immortal master.

The devil was vulnerable when the sun was at its full strength in the sky, she had said, for this was when his power waned. He was defenseless against silver, she had claimed, that most unremarkable of metals, and a silver dagger in his heart would put an end to his eternal life.

And more than that, she had said, for should the Master be slain against all possibility, the boon would be greater than the death of just one demon, even though that demon be the king of hell.

Upon his death, Isavell had said, every demon he ever created would finally be free of the curse that chained them to his will and his magic. They would either return to the mortality so cruelly stripped from them, or they would die, as their master died.

Either outcome was acceptable to Isavell.

Domnall took her at her word, yet Cathal wondered at his judgment. It was clear to any who looked upon him that months of the succubus's ministrations had compromised his physical body as well as his mind. It was not sound.

The villagers whispered that he'd been taken by the devil. Margaret, the witch, looked at him with sad, knowing eyes. His illness was apparent, and his willingness to take Isavell at her word was proof to Cathal that the poison ran deep.

But as Adam had said not four hours before, what choice was left to them? It may well be that the fate of humanity had been delivered into their care the moment Isavell betrayed her creator and divulged the mechanism by which they could destroy him.

And so, as the sun climbed toward its zenith in the first clear sky for more than a fortnight, Cathal was one in their army of six, and together they stormed the monster's lair.

Together they marched to put an end to the terror that stalked them night after night.

Together they made ready to assassinate the overlord of evil and change the world forever.

CHAPTER THREE

It was quiet inside the castle, so they moved carefully, on light feet over moldy, threadbare carpets, and with never a whisper. Adam took the lead, his silver dagger held low. Domnall walked close behind him, his body unnaturally rigid, and Cathal walked in the faint shadows they cast, frightened above anything else.

The building was enormous and ancient, and still home to once-decadent refinement—chaises, tables, rugs, and art in golds and greens and dark reds that hinted of riches but smelled of dust and decay. No fires burned in the hearths—it was cold as night, and the only source of light was where the sun seeped through broken stonework. The air whistled ghostily, giving the impression of unseen residents watching beadily from the shadows, but no others walked the halls.

Cathal's throat was dry, and tears stung his eyes.

Isavell had told them where they would come upon the

Master, that he would be at rest in his chambers in the north wing at noon. They went straight there, too terrified and too determined to even contemplate straying from the main hall to see what else hid behind these walls.

In the north wing, Adam pushed open one heavy timber door, then another, to look into the rooms beyond. Every chamber was different. Some had opulent furniture, now rotted and decrepit. Others were empty and stale. None concealed the demonic overlord, and none hinted at his whereabouts. Not a few held the remains of fallen men, bones that lay undisturbed as evidence of where that one, or that one, had expelled his final breath.

Domnall took no notice at all, but Cathal stopped looking after the second such sight. The other men did the same soon after, and then Adam alone checked if this room, or the next, was the one they sought. Adam's eyes grew tight around the edges, and his lips blanched at each reminder of doom. Cathal thought Adam would have relinquished the duty had there been anyone to take it from him, yet he did not complain.

After an eternity that ended too soon, they reached the Master's room. It was as all the others, large and nondescript, except the far wall had been torn away, opening to a wide, uncovered courtyard, the dirt there damp and dark with the appearance of having been churned under many crossing feet. Cathal wondered fleetingly how the ground could be so wet when the rain had stayed away for such a time.

As Isavell had promised, in the room was a man—only a man—at rest on a wide four-poster bed topped with a mattress that looked as light as clouds and framed with a heavy canopy in faded gold and blue, moldy and foul.

Was he asleep? Cathal could not tell, but his chest rose and fell with deep, measured regularity.

They had no wish to be brave, to confront the devil and offer him leave to defend himself. This was an execution, and though Cathal had often dreamed of challenging an enemy to a contest of courage, he could conjure no regret at their furtiveness now.

The figure on the bed looked a man like any other. His fair face, framed by ink-black hair, was slack with the peace of sleep, and he wore plain, loose linens. Soft, heavy pouches hung from the belt around his waist.

Therein lay his magic. Every story about the Master of Fear described those pouches in precise detail. Inside his pouches was the dust with which he created his demons. Inside his pouches was the power he used to wreak his horror on the world.

Adam crept ahead, one step, then two, and they all did the same until they had circled the bed. Would it really be this simple? Could it be they would murder the king of hell as he lay sleeping? Cathal couldn't believe their good fortune.

And then the figure sat up, opened his dead, black eyes, and smiled like the cat who got the cream.

"Welcome," he purred.

The men said nothing—what words would be enough?— and Cathal was certain further delay would only work in the Master's favor.

He didn't even know his hands had moved until the room was a nightmare come to life.

His knives were sharp, and his aim was true. Cathal threw one blade at the monster's hip, hoping to sever the belt of rope around his waist. The Master hissed at the impact, and his eyes flickered, first to the knife and then to the boy. Rage and recognition burned there.

These men had silver, and that changed everything.

The Master clutched his side and pulled himself out of the bed, fumbling at his pouches with his free hand. The silver had a pronounced effect, and the confirmation that Isavell had spoken the truth exhilarated them.

Cathal's boldness was the provocation they needed to move, and move quickly. He launched his other dagger, and it sliced into the demon's shoulder. The blade struck flesh with the sizzle of meat burning, and the monster bellowed, still trying and failing to access his magic.

Adam moved forward with his silver short-sword held high. The demon abandoned his efforts to open the bags on his belt. He stepped back, and back again, and his face twisted with contempt. Just when Cathal was sure the devil would gather his strength and pounce on them, he turned and fled into the open courtyard.

Domnall was the first to give chase, but they all were out

in the air within seconds. As Cathal ran through the crumbled wall and onto the dirt, he stumbled a little, as did the men beside him, their boots failing to find purchase on the wet, muddy ground. Cathal landed with a grunt as his body hit the earth, and his cheek slid through the slick soil underneath him.

Only with his nose pressed into the filth—as he set his palms into the ground to leverage himself up, as he looked with horror at the viscous muck that stained his skin and caked his shirt—did Cathal understand that the ground was sodden and blackened with blood.

Oh, so much blood.

The Master—Cathal again was disconcerted by how human he looked, how *normal*—turned back to them, standing against what looked to be an altar, enormous and made of stone, and strewn with wicked-looking tools and trappings intended for torture. It was stained with layers upon layers of blood, the old ones dried and black and pitted like the stone, others glistening wetly in the sun.

The air reeked like a slaughterhouse, even without walls and a roof to confine the stench.

Cathal turned his head and vomited. When he raised his eyes, using the back of his arm to wipe clean his mouth, the scene had changed, and his heart beat painfully against his ribs, flying faster and harder than a heart was ever meant to fly.

Domnall moved disturbingly, like a wooden puppet stiff and new to his strings, as the frenetic energy resulting from his drawn-out association with the succubus animated his body with urgent jerks and ghastly resolve. He raised his silver sword and circled his demon nemesis.

Adam joined him, and Cathal felt pulled along, his feet moving of their own will, the cords of their familial blood too strong to leave his father and brother alone exposed to the wrath of the devil. Cathal pulled a second pair of daggers from their hiding places at the top of his boots, and gripped them in his shaking hands, low and tight.

The others became shadows in Cathal's peripheral vision.

The demon lord bared teeth that were bright and clean and unnaturally sharp, and wailed in a way that was both warning and frustration.

Where were his demonic minions? Why was this ruler of unearthly beasts asleep in his den all alone?

Cathal shook off the doubts that threatened to steal away the only shred of courage he could muster and stalked his target as he would stalk a rabbit.

The Master felt at the pouches on his belt, and Cathal waited for him to call out for aid, to unleash his hell hounds, to loose his vampires, but the man clenched his jaw as tightly as he gripped his magic and set his legs against their assault.

Cathal went for the pouches, ducking in low and fast. As Cathal bolted forward, the Master struck out with a bare foot. At the same moment, a sword pierced his left shoulder, and he staggered. Cathal weaved around his flailing body, hunching his shoulder against the painful keening that stretched from the demon's throat, and lashed out with his knife. The blade sliced through the thin rope at his waist as though it were butter, and three of the canvas bags fell to the floor.

Cathal dropped and scooped up the pouches, holding them against his chest as he rolled out of the way. When he'd regained his footing, he stood back in awestruck horror.

Domnall stabbed wildly with his sword, but the Master moved like a snake, avoiding the blade. Adam lunged with a knife, and the Master kicked his wrist, a squeal escaping from between his teeth as his bared skin connected with the silver.

Sean circled wide and came at him from the side, but the altar blocked his way, and the Master jumped back from Sean's approach. He crossed his arms over his chest and curled in on himself as though to protect the target of their campaign. The demon's lips curled back, and he glared at his assailants from under a hooded brow, much like a cornered dog.

They could not do this one move at a time, and as they realized this truth all at once, they were on him like ants over honey. Cathal could no longer see which limbs belonged to whom in the wild disorder. Blades were pulled back and driven in again, yet no blood stained the silver. Desperate to be useful and needing to look away, Cathal returned his daggers to his boots and ripped open the twine that secured the bags of magic. He scattered the dust over the ground, pacing to thoroughly disperse it as it spilled. The dust glimmered, otherworldly, where it settled on the blood-darkened dirt.

Another pouch was flung from the melee, and then another, and another, and yet the stabbing did not stop. Surely, they had reached his heart by now? Cathal dashed in closer to collect the pouches from the ground, and he emptied each one with relief.

Finally, someone—Cathal did not know who—must have pierced the monster's heart, for the body in the center of the fight thrashed uncontrollably, and the sound that escaped his mouth was high and horrid enough that they stopped and covered their ears with their hands. The Master screamed wordlessly, and then, as the men parted to give witness to his death, Cathal saw the single silver stiletto protruding from his chest. Elsewhere on his body, red-hot burns crossed his skin, steaming where the silver had pierced the flesh. Yet still, he spilled no blood.

The devil's shrill cry cut off without warning, and the men held up their weapons as they prepared for him to rally. Instead, he collapsed onto the ground, his fingers clawing at the blood and dirt beneath him. He bellowed unfamiliar words and sounds that were guttural and hateful and loaded with thwarted rage.

He screamed but did not return to his feet, and as his convulsions slowed, so did his voice increasingly lose strength. Soon his words were but mumbles, and his eyes fell closed. And then no sound escaped at all, though his mouth moved to shape the curses he flung their way.

They watched and they waited until the monster was still.

"We have killed the devil," Cathal whispered.

"We have killed the devil!" Adam proclaimed, thrusting his sword over his head.

"Hail, he is dead!" Domnall exulted, for a moment sounding clear of mind, and he danced right there in the mud—in the dirt and the blood and the magic.

It took a moment for them all to understand, to accept that the day had been won, but soon they rejoiced, crowing the hysterical cheers of victors in battle who, having faced an unbeatable enemy, by the grace of God would return home triumphant.

The ground was soft, and it shifted beneath their feet. More than once, someone landed heavily in the muck, but what was muck on your clothes when such joy was to be had? They had killed the Master of Fear, they had delivered salvation to his vampire minions, and they had saved the world!

So easily they forgot that the mess on their skin was a concoction of sacrificial blood and unknown magic.

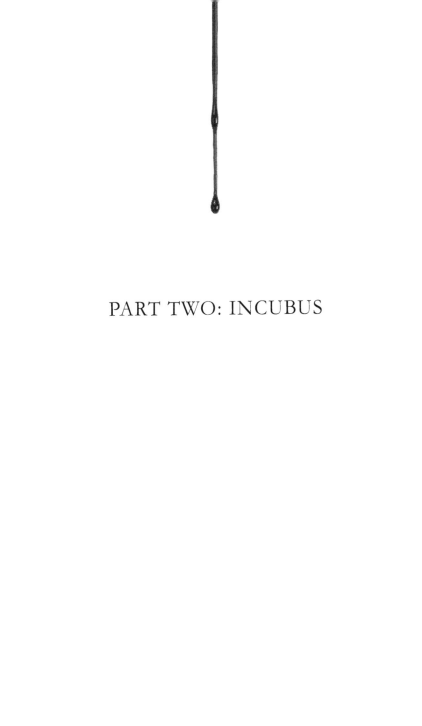

PART TWO: INCUBUS

CHAPTER FOUR

He felt it. The exact moment the Master's heart was impaled, the instant the silver stuck his immortal flesh and froze the breath in his lungs.

Seth felt it, like a tearing that ripped the skin from his body, inch by inch by inch. An agony that began as a silent scream in his ears and reverberated to his toes, peeling the meat from his bones, strip by strip by strip. His throat strangled, too tortured to open and give his pain any voice. His eyes prickled as though he were capable of tears.

Seth wasn't dying, of that he was certain. He was more robust than even his brother and sister vampires. Seth was an incubus—that rare hybrid the Master had created by mistake, an accidental by-product of the devil's repulsive magical experiments. Seth was a drinker of blood as well as a stalker of dreams, a seducer of innocents and a thief of souls. He was tethered to the aether the way the Master was tethered.

If Seth's physical body were pierced, broken, and burned, he had yet hope of resurrection thanks to his phantom soul, that part of him that walked the dream.

So, he wasn't dying, but surely no sentient being, demonic or otherwise, could suffer this level of pain and see the other side of it. It hurt the way nothing had ever hurt, not even his Turning—that never-ending agony of the spell that took his mortal flesh and blood and bone and transmuted it to stone and poison and death.

That was a caress compared to this.

He fell to his knees, crumpled onto the dirt, and braced his arms around his middle to keep the meat from tearing away from his skeleton.

Seth didn't know how long he was down—a minute, an eternity—when the sounds of others moaning, shrieking, and wailing reached his ears. Some of it came on the breeze, calling through the trees around him, layered echoes of pain and grief that began far away. Other screams were close enough Seth could have reached out and touched them.

The forest should have been deathly still, rich with shadows and haunted by invisible evils. New vampires, those most recently Turned, lived in the woods as though they were no better than animals, letting the clothes rot from their backs and relinquishing any attachment to humanity. They hunted like animals, too, sneaking into civilized pockets to snatch what prey they could in those safest hours either side of midnight, and occasionally killing each other for sport.

Seth sympathized with them, for his first decades of this existence reflected too closely the behaviors of the wretches he now avoided, but that wasn't his life. Not anymore. Speed and stealth weren't so necessary when one had heightened senses and the power of seduction at one's fingertips.

Seth had been a vampire for eighty-seven years—and a human for one day short of eighteen years before that—and with his family, together sacrificed at the same Turning, he embraced a more civilized way of being. True, they had lived like savages for years, in the beginning not understanding what the urges were that pulsed through their changed bodies, unprepared for the way stolen blood would cyclically thicken and slow in their systems until desiccation threatened, only to be relieved by satiating themselves with the life of a living creature. An animal would do, they had learned eventually, but human blood was a prize like none other.

At first, the thirst had assaulted them daily, but as time passed, the desperation thinned. Now, nearly a century later, Seth could stretch for weeks, sometimes months, between meals. He did not grow older in the traditional sense, his body did not change in a way anybody could measure, but as his system adjusted and decelerated, he did not need to feed as often as younger demonic spawn.

And though blood was beautiful, Seth's other hungers were more pressing, and he had other desires he'd indulge before more obvious rewards. There weren't many like Seth— the incubus, or the female succubus—who fed off souls as well as blood, but for one such as he, who could step into mortal dreams and, through them, play freely in the aether, there was no greater high, no more ecstatic pleasure, than the capture of that most sacred mortal essence: the soul.

Even in his tortured hurt, he shivered involuntarily at the memory of such raw pleasure. It had been a long time since that ecstasy had been his, but he had never forgotten the way it felt, and now he beat back the overwhelming urge to seek out a victim to assuage his pain.

He was a creature designed for gratification. He was not built to endure distress.

So, the sounds of demons dying were incredible. The agony in his body was shocking. That he could recall pleasure among it all was abhorrent and gruesome testimony of his corrupted heart. He was a monster, and he should have broken by now, and yet there was something in him that forced him to hands and knees, pushed him forward one inch, then another, to seek out the source of the sounds.

He dragged himself out of the trees and to the knoll at the edge of the woods, where he looked down over the town.

Hundreds of vampires were loose in the streets, keening in grief and howling with rage. Pitiful bleats punctuated the demonic cacophony, marking the deaths of terrorized humans. The air was perfumed with fresh blood and fear-sweat, the stink of entrails spilled onto the ground, and the earthy tones of dirt and stone kicked up by the frantic footfalls of humans running and demons giving chase.

It was a massacre. No pretense made at secrecy. Nowhere evidence of seduction.

The vampires had gone mad.

CHAPTER FIVE

No demon created by the Master of Fear ever roamed far from him after their Turning. He had a...*resonance*... that left his progeny high and heady, and it was difficult to leave his orbit. But vampires were hardly civil, choosing to work alone or with kin unless compelled to do otherwise, and now so many of all those in existence had descended upon the town.

As the humans squalled and ran for houses that could not protect them, the vampires lashed out with reflexes too fast to be God-given. They tore apart those soft, wet bodies and ducked their heads lustily, greedily, into hot, exposed flesh. Even from this distance, Seth's ears picked out the luscious suck of blood being pulled from veins still thumping. And where the vampire fed, he left a body in the dirt or on the stones before moving on to the next.

Seth searched with darting glances for his family—his

mother, father, sister, brothers—but could not find them among the demonic berserkers. Even in his pain, he found a kernel of hope they were not participants in this, the most revolting of riots.

It took little effort to understand that whatever bond he had with the Master had ruptured abruptly and violently not half an hour earlier, but where Seth suffered deep physiological and metaphysical pain, the fracture had had a very different effect on the others of his kind.

Seth watched on, mortified. Even at night, when they ruled the world, vampires were never this reckless in their hunting. The sun weakened them and it was uncomfortable to be in its light, the sensation of relative weakness palpable and disconcerting, so vampires walked the world under the cover of darkness, when their strength was at its peak. The only exceptions were desperate demons who had not fed enough in the night hours and juvenile vampires whose thirst was too great to wait for the sun to go down to slake.

But today, the Master's monsters were bereft of control. They had lost any sense of self-preservation, had abandoned every instinct to hide and hunt in the shadows.

Seth stood and forced his body to move against explosions of pain. He needed to find his family. They, too, could be among the townsfolk, killing indiscriminately and uncontrollably, and that was not their way.

Was it his phantom soul that protected him from the madness? And if so, what did that mean for his kin who did not possess the same? When this darkness lifted from their minds, they would feel shame and guilt at the way they had behaved, even involuntarily.

It had only been a score of years since Seth's parents had felt the rebirth of humanity deep within and had begun to abstain from traditional pleasures. Seth, his brothers, and his sister followed their example. On occasion, they'd even come to love the mortals they preyed upon. They'd dedicated themselves to alternative ways of living, ways that weren't so corrupt. It had become easier each day, each year, to go without, until some moments it was almost as though they'd broken free of their cursed existence.

Determined to save his loved ones from themselves, Seth walked into the town, his arms wrapped around his torso as though they could keep his entrails from falling free.

Around him, vampires lurched at human throats with a desperation Seth had not seen before. With no charade of affection or pleasure, they applied their lips to throbbing arteries, sunk their subtly sharpened canines into delicate skin stretched thin over wildly fragrant carotids. It was a sensual experience, one to be prolonged and savored, but there was no delay today. Vampires sucked bodies dry in a matter of seconds and flung them away as though they were nothing but rags—men, women, children all.

Seth shouldered his way past demon after demon as they clawed past him, seeking victims. There was no lucidity in their gazes, no way to reach them even had Seth wanted to try.

Would there be an end to any of this, or did the end of their creator mean eternal pain? Eternal madness? Was this the future of demons and humanity? The fate of the very world?

No, that was not something he wanted to dwell upon. He needed to find his parents. His mother would know how to soothe his fears. His father would have a plan.

The more he forced his muscles to move, the more the agony seemed to ease. He quickened his step, arms still wrapped around his body, and occasionally staggering as the pain dug deep into his chest. More than once, he sought out traces of familiar scents but quickly pulled back. The fresh blood called to him too strongly, and he was tempted to take some for himself, just this once, just to soothe the pressure that shot through his hardened muscles and altered veins. It was a superhuman feat to keep moving without stepping aside to enter a dream and steal a soul. Again, he shivered with desire.

His focus shifted frantically, but his family was nowhere amid the violence. Seth found it somewhere in himself to give thanks that somehow they may have found the strength of will to restrain themselves. Hope straightened his back, and the pain seemed to ease a fraction more.

CHAPTER SIX

Seth made his way back to the trees, intending to skirt the southern border of the woods and complete a circuit of the town before heading deeper into the forest. He ran parallel to the common road when the disconcerting sounds of men whooping and singing came toward him from the north. Instinctively, he scaled the tree beside him and waited.

There were six men, plainly dressed, their sun-darkened skin and worn clothes caked with dry blood and dirt. As the sun shone over them, Seth picked out the glimmer of magic on their bodies just as the light glinted off the silver at their hips.

He gripped the boughs over his head, his fingers making divots in the wood.

Seth prepared to drop onto them, to rub the magic from their clothes, to lick the blood and dust from their skin and consume the magic they so flagrantly wore for the world to see. Where had they found it?

Seth knew the answer, of course. There was only one source of magic, and, partnered with the weapons made of silver, he understood with sudden, terrifying clarity what must have happened.

Impossibly, these ordinary men had slain his creator.

Seth felt both awed and aggrieved, equally grateful and murderous. His fingers dug deeper into the tree, that one action the only thing keeping him from pouncing upon the men, to take their lives and retrieve the stolen magic.

At this distance from the town, they should have been too far to hear the sounds of death and violence there. They could have no knowledge of the nightmare that awaited them, and it would be another ten minutes at the pace they were moving before they would pick up the wailing on the wind. And yet as the last man passed him—a boy, really, no more than fifteen—their chins lifted, a pack of wolves pricking their ears at a signal of distress, and as a single body, they shot forward, as fast as a stone flies free from a catapult.

They moved with a speed to which Seth was accustomed—a speed normally reserved for creatures of his supernatural ilk. In fact, at this time of day, when the sun was high, Seth was uncomfortably unsure he could have bested them in a contest back to the town.

It only took a split second for Seth to decide that he must follow. His family would need to be fine for a while longer.

Seth sped after them, taking no pains to conceal himself. Ninety seconds later, he pulled up short, spying the men standing stunned at the edge of the horror, on the same knoll where Seth himself had first surveyed the carnage.

His brain worked faster than even the cleverest human, but Seth still could not understand what he saw next.

The men exchanged not a word before, again, they surged forward at an inconceivable rate, descending on the town as though they had the reinforcements of six hundred men behind them. They ran with the power of men fueled by rage and adrenaline—but no amount of rage or adrenaline could explain away their speed.

They would be massacred along with the rest of the townsfolk, but Seth could not look away, for he knew the end would not be as he expected.

Immediately, he was proven right, and a massacre of another kind began.

CHAPTER SEVEN

It had been many, many decades since Seth had felt so uncertain of his existence. What in the world could unbalance a vampire?

Now, he had the answer to that question.

The six men with magic on their skin pulled free the weapons at their waists—long swords and short, throwing knives and daggers—and without a moment's pause, threw themselves into the chaos. Quickly, by force or by design, they separated.

That should have been the end of them.

It wasn't.

The first warrior—for warrior he was—confronted a demon in the middle of its meal. With a roar of rage, the man pulled the vampire off the human—too late to save the latter—and with inexplicable strength, hurled the monster into the side of a building. The force was great enough that the demon landed with a thud, stunned at the ferocity of the impossible attack. Before the vampire could get his feet under him, the warrior plunged his sword deep into its chest.

The strike was true. The tip of the blade pushed repulsively out of the demon's back, wet with the blood the vampire had stolen in its rampage. The demon sagged against the sword, heart skewered.

Killed instantly.

Had the blade missed the center of that vital organ, even by a hairsbreadth, the vampire would have healed with time. As it was, nothing could return that ghoul to its pathetic existence now.

Good.

Seth shook off the meandering thought as he watched the man, unable to dislodge the weapon after a firm tug on the hilt, place a booted foot against the vampire's chest and kick him loose. The vampire slid off the blade and slumped into a small pool of blood.

The body must have been so bloated with liquid to be releasing anything in death. Seth had seen nothing like it. Dead demons were usually dry husks, broken and pulled apart by a rival for a meal or conquest. Vampires replete with stolen blood were strong. Unbeatable.

Unkillable.

Immortal.

The warrior moved on to another foe. This time, the vampire moved quickly enough to swipe at the man, lashing out with fingers so strong they should have torn the muscles from the man's bones.

And the warrior didn't flinch.

The demon was taken by the throat. She clawed at the arm that held her aloft, leaving scratches in the man's skin but eliciting not a whimper. The human who would have been the vampire's next victim fell to the ground and huddled there with her arms around her head. From nowhere Seth could place, a throwing knife appeared in the back of the vampire, the blade sunk hilt-deep, left of the spine. The warrior dropped the demon, and she collapsed into the dirt.

Seth couldn't be certain at this angle, but there was a good chance that this knife, too, had met its target. Straight through the heart, and another demon down.

Seth tore his eyes away from that first man and searched out those who had marched with him. One, two, three, four…All felled vampires with an energy that matched the frenzied horror of the demons and with strength and speed that far surpassed it.

It could not be true, but the men had magic, and that magic made them something other than men.

The humans who thought to run and hide from the vampires were now successfully finding refuge behind closed doors as the slayers decimated the demonic ranks. The demons were distracted and selfish, and it never occurred to them to set aside their prey and combine their defense to meet and defeat the threat. Though truthfully,

Seth was not sure a concerted effort would have been enough to beat back those men.

Seth scanned the town again, wondering if the sixth man had been defeated. Was it possible that a vampire could best one of these warriors?

Four seconds later, Seth spotted the man, red hair matted, clothes and skin glittering unnaturally in the sunlight, running toward the shadows of the forest. It made little sense to Seth, but he abandoned any curiosity at the sound of running footsteps approaching from behind.

A quick test of the air, and a little of the tension leached from Seth's body. He didn't turn to greet the newcomer but could now watch the performance before him with less stress, more awe. It truly was miraculous, and Seth would not grieve the demise of the monsters there.

"What do you make of it?" a deep voice asked.

"I hardly know," Seth replied. "Are you all right?"

"It hurts a little," Leo replied flatly, "but aye, I am all right."

"Father? Mother?" Seth asked, still distracted. "Felicity?" He didn't think to enquire after Noel. Had Leo's twin been in any danger, Leo would not have been so calm.

Silence met his question, where Seth anticipated an easy reply.

Had there been fresh, hot blood in his body, had he not already been the temperature of frost, Seth would have shivered as cold as the grave.

"What is it, Leo?"

"Father is with Noel and Felicity at the far eastern border of the endless woods. When…this…began"—Noel waved his hand toward the town but didn't look upon it, distaste apparent in the twist of his mouth—"we four were together. We sensed the fall of the Master, of course, and yet didn't succumb the way the others succumbed." He eyed Seth appraisingly but asked him no questions, and for that, Seth was grateful. "When the violence became too great, we fled. Mother…We do not know where she is. She was not with us when this began. Father is desperate to search for her, but…." Leo grimaced.

Seth prompted him impatiently. "What would delay him?"

Leo rubbed his face in a show of impossible weariness. "Noel and Felicity collected two strays along the way."

Seth was growing impatient at having to pull the story from Leo piece by piece. He did his best to soften his tone, but his frustration was plain.

"Strays?" he asked. "Humans?"

It wouldn't be the first time Felicity had taken a mortal for a pet. Their parents discouraged it, but, unavoidably, the humans were only too happy—nay, desperate—to follow her around the way an obedient dog chases its master and begs for scraps. Seth couldn't understand the relevance now, or Leo's hesitancy, when so much else was more urgent.

"Nay. Vampires."

This caught Seth's attention. He deliberately ignored the

horror unfolding in the town and gave Leo his full attention.

"*Vampires?* Today?"

Leo nodded, for the first time glancing at the slaughter below, but refusing to linger there.

"A brother and sister, recently Turned and feral, but when their family fell upon the town with the others, these two… did not. We cannot understand why yet, but Noel and Felicity insist we take them in until we can ask them their reasons." Leo rolled his shoulders. "It matters little to me, but it delays our search for Mother."

Seth nodded, hearing the unspoken meaning of Leo's words. If Noel wanted this, Leo would support it. Seth's brothers were cut from the same cloth, connected in a way other siblings were not. Seth was just as much their brother, but he didn't share their telepathic conversations or uncanny mannerisms. They differed only by their preference in prey.

"I can search for her. She cannot be far. Tell Father I will join you soon."

Seth refused to acknowledge the worm of fear that suddenly burrowed in his gut.

Leo merely nodded as though a positive outcome was the foregone conclusion, and his confidence gave Seth hope.

They were vampires. He was an incubus.

Unbreakable.

Unkillable.

Immortal.

Seth refused to look down upon the town again.

"Has Father any ideas on why we are not…affected…as the others are?"

Leo nodded thoughtfully. "He suspects our abstinence has weakened our bonds with the Master. His death does not feel so unbearable to us."

Seth wondered at his father's insight, but the rationale was sound.

As Leo sped away and disappeared into the trees, Seth picked up his circuit of the town, crossing the trail of the warrior who had fled into the woods and deciding on a whim to follow it.

His thoughts focused on his mother.

Would she have felt pain as Seth had felt pain? Would the severance have affected her in much the same way? He shuddered to think of his mother enduring that never-ending agony. She was too good for that, too undeserving.

Seth ran on, shying away from the picture of a future in which the Master was gone and, in his place, magical men who could murder demons walked freely over the Earth.

PART THREE: WITCH

CHAPTER EIGHT

Margaret knew today would be the day she would slay the devil, but she knew not how that could be true.

It dawned a morning like any other, until she saw the cloud cover had broken for the first time in a fortnight. For fourteen days, it had hulked gray and heavy over the land, never opening to water the ground, ominous and refusing to move.

Until that day, when the sun rose, and the horizon brightened, and the heavens were a clear, brilliant blue.

That blue told Margaret her dream would come true.

The first indication of strife arrived on the wind, wails and howls and cries and screams from direction of the town.

They chilled her blood, those screams.

Margaret kept her home on the very southern end of town, as far enough away as she could be from her neighbors and still claim to live in the village, so she heard the violence clearly, and knew evil was at work in the streets.

She stayed inside, protected by wards and charms.

After a time, the sounds changed to shouts and bellows of rebellion in human voices that should not have been able to rise in strength as they did. They were teamed with the keening of stone-hard bodies being broken and torn, the wet ripping of bloated hearts being pierced with silver blades.

Ah.

Margaret had always known silver could kill a vampire, but what good was that knowledge when no human was strong enough or fast enough to get near enough to the demons to use it? Silver or no, a mortal would be dead on the instant should he try to approach this enemy.

The knowledge of silver was all well and good, but it had never been of any benefit to her.

Yet now, someone had succeeded where she could not. The riddle did not bother her. She would know the how and the why of it soon enough.

Margaret waited.

After a time, the world was silent again. Margaret's daughter, Kateryn, knew her mother had woken anxious that day and had been distracted well before the slaughter began, but Margaret had not yet shared the true reason why. Let Kateryn think her worry was grounded in the stunning deaths of the vampires outside. It was not a far stretch of the imagination, by any means.

The quiet went on.

Five minutes.

Ten.

Fifteen.

Margaret jumped at desperate pounding on her timber door, a fist thumping the wood with an urgency even the ungifted could have sensed.

Kateryn looked to Margaret with steady grey eyes, her distress only visible in the slight crease of her brow and the set of her mouth. She placed the dress she was darning on the table, folded her hands on her lap, and watched.

Margaret opened the door, and had she been less practiced, she would have stepped back in horror, but she had already gathered her wits and her mystery about her, so she barely swayed. She even managed to scowl a little. "What do ye want?"

The man before her swallowed nervously, the fists that had hammered the door now balled up by his sides. His eyes and hair were wild. "We seek assistance."

Margaret looked over his shoulder to the others behind him: four more, one much older, the youngest barely fourteen, all with that same mad look about the eyes. The men had the semblance of family about them, with their varied shades of red-gold hair and all sporting broad shoulders. Margaret recognized them and noted that Domnall was missing. She fought to suppress a shake of her head. The pieces were assembling.

"Quick, inside with you, then. Move along." Margaret waved them in, putting on a show of bad humor—it's what they expected, dealing with her. Widowed old women who healed the ill and dealt in charms had reputations to maintain, after all.

Margaret swept her gaze over the street outside. It was empty and unnaturally calm. A curtain twitched in the nearest house, then was still, and in the distance, a body lay abandoned on the road. Margaret closed the door firmly and turned back to her visitors.

They stood in a ragged line, faces pale and yet, somehow, bright with vigor. Margaret felt the magic pulsing on them, and she grasped her hands behind her back as a reminder to herself to be patient.

"Care to explain yourselves?" she demanded roughly, though by now she was sure she knew the answer.

It appeared the first man had taken the lead, and he was the one who answered.

"Father told us…he said…."

Margaret suddenly recalled the man's name. Adam. His wife had sought her out just last month. She could not get with child, poor lass, after two years of trying. There were herbs for that, of course, and charms. It was an easy enough heartache to fix, and Margaret was confident they'd be blessed with a babe within the year.

Speared by Margaret's cool blue eyes, Adam stumbled over his words until he trailed off altogether, staring into his open palms. Nobody could miss the glittering sheen between the dirt and dust and sweat and blood on his skin.

Margaret's fingers itched. No use in waiting any longer. There was work to do.

She bustled to the hearth, where she kept a basket of those tools and accouterments of her craft that weren't so suspicious. From there, she selected a tiny brush with fine, stiff bristles, and a canvas pouch, light but tightly woven. She didn't explain herself, but as she set about brushing the men inch by inch, painstakingly sweeping every remnant of magic into the pouch she held open in her hand, they seemed to find relief in her authority and action. Perhaps they believed this would cure whatever ailed them.

Margaret would not—could not—give any promises, but her silence and industriousness loosened their tongues.

"Father was certain a silver knife would kill the Master," Adam explained, eagerly now, standing uncannily still while the old woman worked. This would take too long, she realized. She waved a hand to Kateryn. The other woman found a brush and a pouch, but, at the click of Margaret's tongue and an impatient shake of her head, Kateryn replaced the pouch with a battered silver bowl.

Margaret would store all the magic in her pouch, not risk losing a speck of it to the fabric of the other.

Adam had stopped talking, and Margaret grunted. "Where would Domnall get an idea like that?"

"Isavell," he mumbled, unwilling to confess but unable to dissemble.

"And where is Domnall now?"

Adam exchanged a quick look with the youngest boy, who dropped his eyes, and then answered. "He disappeared into the woods. I thought it best to let him go."

Margaret said nothing. She would pass no judgment. Domnall's penance had been set the moment he consented to bed a demon.

Kateryn interjected. They often managed people this way—a little honey to counteract the stick. It worked well, and it helped that Kateryn was lovely to look at. "And what happened next? You look as though you've had quite the adventure."

It was the young man who answered, with equal measures of fear and wonder in his unreliable, cracking baritone. Margaret did her best to appear nonplussed as the boy wound out the events of the day, tried her hardest to behave as though what he shared was the style of story she'd heard many times before, but her heart stopped more than once, her mouth dried enough to make swallowing painful, and she saw Kateryn's hand shake as it carefully dislodged the magic from skin and cloth.

The boy's tale was one for the ages.

CHAPTER NINE

They had found the Master of Fear, he said, in repose in his castle on the northern side of the woods. He'd woken and run; they'd given chase and slain him.

The devil hadn't bled, he recalled, and had refused to die until the silver had struck true into his cold, stone heart.

They had danced in the bloodied dirt and laughed while the devil screamed words beyond understanding and writhed in the throes of his death.

They left his body in the dirt in the place where it had fallen, to become carrion for the birds and bones for the wolves.

Margaret's brush paused at this part of their story, but only Kateryn noted it. Margaret returned to her sweeping, avoiding her daughter's stare and the concern shining there.

They had returned home with the thrill of triumph racing through their veins. They'd sung and cheered and exulted in the glory of having done what no man had ever been able to do. What a hero's welcome awaited them!

And then, they'd heard the heartrending sounds of people dying. Shrieks and screams and despair on the wind. The heavy, dusty thuds of corpses hitting the ground. The wet pull of blood siphoned from open veins, and the gurgle of it slipping down greedy, open gullets.

White-hot rage had ignited their blood, clouded their minds and driven all rational thought from their heads. Instinctively, they'd run toward the sounds, no strategy clear until the scene before them compelled them to act.

The memories of what happened next were…hazy.

They'd drawn their weapons, those blades cast in silver, and fallen on the evil hordes. The vampires had been distracted, too thirsty or too arrogant to be wary of the six silly human males trying to stop them—but those silly human males never thought twice about what needed to be done.

And just as their master had, those demons felt the sting of the silver, weakening them where it connected with skin.

Killing them where it connected with the heart.

Over and over, they separated vampire from human, sometimes too late to mete out anything other than vengeance, other times gratefully in time to save a victim from a death so foul as to be bled dry by a monster. Soon, the mortals were in danger no longer. They were saved!

The town fell still, and the men waited for their reception. But the people could not see the goodness of their saviors, and they ran from the slayers as they would run from vampires, their fear declaring they recognized little difference between their murderers and liberators. All were terrifying, violent, and powerful beyond explanation.

And that they were, the slayers realized, once the demons were dead or fled. They were violent, like the vampire. Strong like him, and fast, with ears that picked up the almost-silent sounds of feet speeding away through the forest, and noses too sensitive to the smells of entrails and human waste that coated the streets, and eyes too keen to the sight of flesh torn and discarded as though it were refuse.

They were more than demons, yet still less. They were stronger than the vampire, and faster than him too, with better senses and more exact movements. But their flesh was soft, as a man's flesh was soft, their pulses still thumped in their necks and their wrists, their eyes still shone green and brown and gold with not a hint of black.

Yes. They were more than demons, and less.

The young boy stopped talking, and the men waited for Margaret to explain what had changed them so. Only a witch could tell them what they were now.

Margaret felt the weight of their expectation. She laboriously pushed herself from her knees to her feet, Kateryn offering her an arm for support. Margaret said nothing right away.

She knew what had happened—it was all too clear to her—but it was not a truth she expected these men to embrace.

Giving each of the five slayers a last look-over, searching for any spot of magic she might have missed and finding the results the best she could hope for, she trussed the drawstrings of the pouch and attached it to her belt.

"Undress. Leave your clothes. I shall have them burned. Kateryn, please fetch wash water and blankets."

"Have you cured us?" the older boy asked, the hope in his voice causing Margaret physical pain.

She pretended not to hear him.

People had too much faith in her and what she could do. Aye, she preferred it that way—encouraging their awe was a good way to head off an argument, and a little fear worked to her advantage—but there were some rare occasions she felt a fraud.

Her fingers brushed the pouch at her waist.

Kateryn followed her instructions efficiently, and the men obeyed with alacrity. Soon, there was a pile of filthy ragged fabrics on the floor and a bucket of cloudy, red-stained water in the corner. When all had been done to her satisfaction, Margaret bade the men sit.

"Young Adam," she said, doing her best to control the gruffness in her voice. She intuitively knew that, though he was not the oldest of the group, Adam would lead them, so she looked at him as she spoke. "The Master of Fear has cursed you."

The intakes of breath around her were sharp. One man wept, then another, but she refused to feel pity.

It was a harsh truth that some and not others were destined for magic. She herself had had no choice when the dream called to her, and her daughters ever after would share her gifts. It was a burden that must be borne, and no use wishing it otherwise.

"The blood on the ground, the magic on your skin, his screams as he died," Margaret reminded them, and the light of understanding brightened Adam's face. "You have been given a…gift, the power of the demon. I suspect it was the devil's intention to corrupt your hearts as well as your bodies, but either his evil was too weak, or your intention was too pure, and in that—thank heavens—he failed."

She wished she could have given them time to accept their fate, but common sense and experience told her men responded better to orders and action, and there was no time to wait anyway. The day was not yet done. They all had work to do, Margaret among them.

"We cannot rest yet," she told them, and their heads jerked up. "You have slain these demons with silver, but that is not enough, for the undead can be resurrected. Return now to the streets and burn the bodies, then inter the ashes in urns and caskets of silver, to be buried under a foot of dirt."

When the men did not move, when they did not hear her words, she put a hand on Adam's shoulder to call him back to the room.

"Adam," she said firmly. "The demons are not yet dead. They will rise again, and only you can stop them." Her voice dropped low, insistent, for his ears only. "The devil did not curse your heart. That, in its entirety, still belongs to you."

Adam's nod was, at first, absent, until finally his brows drew down and his body shivered as though he could shake away his dark thoughts.

"Witch, we hear you. We will go back into the streets and collect the bodies for burning. We cannot permit the demons to rise again."

Margaret nodded, riding high on a surge of relief that Adam hadn't realized the true import of her words. The last part of her plan was hers to execute, and hers alone.

And then the young one cried out.

"But the Master of Fear! We left his body there, in the dirt and the blood!"

Adam stood abruptly, his blanket slipping as his mind fumbled toward the understanding Margaret had wished to keep for herself. Kateryn modestly dropped her eyes, but Margaret enjoyed looking at the young man's muscular figure before she stooped to retrieve the covering for him.

"The Master is mine," she said, again brushing the pouch of magic. "He is not like the creatures he makes, as easily vanquished with silver and flame. His death requires something...more."

Kateryn walked to a window and moved the curtain aside. "Mother, the day is too far gone. You cannot leave now."

Margaret retrieved her cloak from the hook by the door and swung it 'round her shoulders. "I can, and I must. Do not fret, Kateryn, for I have seen it in the dream. This is my task to complete."

Kateryn knew better than to argue in front of company, and Margaret relied on her good manners to tie her tongue long enough to leave her behind. What she hadn't expected was the chivalrous nature of her guests.

"Nay, witch, you cannot go to the castle alone," Adam declared, recalling his decency and clutching the blanket to him. "Any vampires that remain will come out again in the night. If you set out immediately, you still will not reach the Master's lair until sundown, and you'll be required to return by the moon. The risk is too great."

Kateryn fervently nodded her agreement.

Margaret hitched her cloak irritably. She detested being told what to do—not that there was occasion for it to happen often. Indeed, she could not recall the last time anyone had attempted to thwart her wishes. It was one advantage of being old and mysterious and, apparently, all-knowing.

"This thing I must do, I must do alone," she repeated testily.

"I will escort you to the doors of the castle," Adam replied. "I will not interfere with your task, only see that you arrive there and return home safely. Please, you must allow this."

Margaret refused to look at the worry in Kateryn's face, but she felt the weight of it all the same.

"Very well," she replied tightly. "There are clothes you can wear in the trunk over there"—remnants of her dead husband's wardrobe she'd been too sentimental to give away—"but I will not wait for you. You can follow on the road."

Margaret opened the door, beginning her journey with a straight back and no rearward glance. She heard Adam giving orders to collect the demon corpses and build a pyre on which to burn them. Kateryn knew where to find silver urns to inter the ashes. They had no further need of Margaret.

She set the minor worries of the men and the dead demons from her mind and firmed her resolve. She had the magic, and the dream had shown her how to use it. The time had come.

Today, she would kill the devil.

CHAPTER TEN

It did not take very long for Adam to join her on the road, but still, she was past the town and walking under the majestic trees of the endless woods by the time he approached. He slowed his pace and walked a half step behind. Margaret nodded infinitesimally to acknowledge his presence.

Margaret's husband had not been as large a man as Adam, and the clothes he wore were ill-fitting, especially around his broad shoulders and shapely calves, but it was of inconsiderable matter today. Margaret couldn't bring herself to care about it further than to note it fleetingly. The slayer was again armed with his silver sword, and he also had a silver chain looped loosely around one shoulder and a silver talisman hanging from his neck. Kateryn must have furnished him with it before he took his leave. She was a quick woman.

Margaret returned her attention to the path ahead—both literally and figuratively—and they walked some way in silence. She felt no need to fill the air with chatter, her determination was so fixed on her end point, but before long, Adam spoke. "Witch, I confess my desire to escort you to the castle is not selfless. I wish to speak with you."

Margaret grunted noncommittally.

She knew well that her magic and the gifts that came with it—the abilities to tell fortunes, dispense herbs and hedge medicines, coax babies into wombs, and curse unfaithful husbands—required service to others, and it was for this reason that her sour disposition was one she carefully cultivated. She hadn't always been that way.

The younger Margaret had been a more open, welcoming woman, eager to please and desperate to help, but her magic was not fail-safe, and too many of those who took her charms and potions misused them and spoiled their magic. Soon, dissatisfied customers had little hesitation abusing a lass they considered weak and vulnerable. In time, she'd learned to couch her offers in threats of retraction and warnings of failure, wearing a constant mask of peevishness and never volunteering her magic or herself, under any circumstances. Fewer people came to her, now, and those who did considered her their final hope. They took what she offered, no matter how meager, and were grateful for it.

Things worked more efficiently when people were too afraid of her to argue, and it was better this way, safer—for her, and for Kateryn.

But she recognized the inflection in Adam's voice, had

heard the same many times before, and could tell he wanted something from her. She wouldn't give it up willingly.

"I worry for us," he began. "Your explanation, if you'll pardon my bluntness, is too thin to provide comfort."

Far from offended, Margaret appreciated the man's forthrightness. It gave her the space to speak similarly. "It is all I can offer you. What you are, and what you will be, is for you to discover."

"Surely there is more you can tell us? What do ordinary men know about magic?" He shook his head, his sadness palpable, and it struck Margaret how young he was, but she couldn't afford to sympathize too greatly.

"Adam, no," she repeated. "I wish it were different, but you will need to tread your own path. Find comfort in the fact that you have brothers beside you, and you do not do it alone."

The remainder of their journey passed without further conversation. As they drew closer to the castle, unfamiliar waves of fear and nervous energy threatened to drown Margaret. She beat them back with determined grit and enthusiasm for her task. Only she could do what needed to be done, and afterward…well, the world would be very different for them all, and her gifts would have served an everlasting purpose.

The dream had been clear.

Without his magic, the Master was nothing—merely a bloodless man who could not be killed. Without the magic Margaret now so possessively grasped, he had no power of his own.

In the dream, she'd seen herself stand over the devil as he lay slain, open the pouch of magic, and dip her hand into the dust. With her palm and fingers coated with power, she'd thrust her hand deep into the demon's chest and gripped his dead heart. Then, she'd entered the aether through sleep, dragging the soul of the devil into the dream with her, and there, she'd vanquished him absolutely, pushing him out into the oblivion beyond the void.

Only destruction this complete could rid the world of this monster, the father of vampires and the creator of hell.

Only Margaret, witch and walker of dreams, had the ability to see it done.

Adam refused to leave her at the doors to the castle, as he had promised to do, and she stifled her exasperation. It would not do to expend energy on this detail when such a great demand lay ahead. He led the way to the Master's chambers and insisted on entering before her, sword drawn, to ensure it was safe.

He returned swiftly, a look of puzzlement on his face that gave Margaret pause.

"He is not there," he told her.

"Nonsense," she snapped and brushed past him into the room.

She walked around the large bed and out to the courtyard beyond, recalling from their story that this was where the

Master had fallen. And yes, there was the altar and fresh scuff marks in the dirt, but nowhere could she spy a body.

The Master was gone.

For a moment, Margaret imagined that he had risen, that so quickly his body had healed, and even now, he lay in wait in the shadows to seek his vengeance. But as the panic settled, she understood her fear was talking, not her good sense. It was too soon for him to have recovered his physical strength.

She detached the pouch of magic from her belt and gripped it in her fist.

She was certain the devil would not risk walking Earth without his magic. His monumental ego would not allow it, for bereft of it, he had no means to create his minions, no authority over demons and mortals alike. He was but a man—albeit an immortal one—and he would be damned to spend his entire existence without power or purpose, supernatural or otherwise. The devil was too mad and too ambitious to settle for that.

No. Now Margaret was entirely sure, as she looked around his repulsive sacrificial grounds and fought back the urge to vomit, that he would not return to his Earth-bound body until the magic was again in his possession. Then he could live as he always had done—with absolute domination rooted in great evil. While he waited for the right moment to return, his essence would hide in the aether.

This meant someone—a demon—had found the body and spirited it away, for reasons known only unto him.

Margaret could not think what to do next. The dream had not prepared her to be thwarted. Panic tightened her chest.

A sharp squeal of pain put an end to those thoughts, and Margaret turned to see Adam squaring up to battle a vampire.

CHAPTER ELEVEN

He had lashed out at it with the chain Kateryn had given him, and the touch of silver against the demon's flesh had elicited the screech. Margaret squinted a little, noting the creeping dimness. The sun was almost beyond the horizon, casting the room in shadows. Darkness would soon fall.

Adam pointed the tip of his short-sword at the demon's chest. The vampire, rolling her eyes like a crazed animal, screamed her pain and frustration. Too fast for Margaret to follow, the demon folded her body out of the way of the silver blade and lunged for her attacker, swiping low in an effort to take his legs out from under him.

Confident the supernaturally gifted slayer could outmaneuver the monster easily, Margaret's hand flew to her mouth when the man slammed heavily to the ground, rolling away only just in time to avoid the impact of the vampire's incoming open palm to his face. Instead, it connected with the floor, fracturing the stone with a shocking crack.

Adam was not deterred. He sprung to his feet again with his jaw set determinedly and his eyes as focused as the vampire's were fitful.

Margaret stepped away, her foot crunching the debris under her boot. At the faint noise, Adam flung out an arm as though to hold her back from interfering, but he didn't turn to make sure she obeyed. His attention was on the demon.

Margaret wondered briefly if she should, in fact, get involved. She held the pouch of magic protectively against her chest, her thumb stroking the fabric as she considered dipping her fingers into the powder and using it to confront the vampire. It might work, only she had no real concept of how to use it other than what the dream had shown her, and there was no guarantee that what would debilitate the Master would do the same for one of his creations.

Margaret imagined confronting the demon with nothing more than a hand laden with magic, attempting to reach into her chest to rip out the heart, and the vampire brushing her away, crushing her with as much effort as it would take to swat a fly, her body broken on the floor, the blood sucked from her veins, weakening her until…

The impulse to intervene left her as abruptly as it had taken hold.

It would be a last resort, she decided. She was not a soldier in the traditional sense. Her gifts were of the aether.

These physical conflicts were better left to those outfitted to manage them.

So, Margaret stood there, a horrified yet wondering spectator, as she witnessed this almost unprecedented of battles. Only 'almost,' for this confrontation had happened many times in the town not half a day earlier. It was the first time, however, that she saw for herself the power and capabilities of these newly minted vampire slayers.

The demon rocked on her toes, her feral eyes wary, as she realized it was no ordinary human before her. The silver weapons were one thing; a mortal capable of withstanding her strength was altogether another.

Adam did not wait for her to attack again. He feinted one way and then the other. Their reflexes were equally matched, and the vampire easily avoided the thrusts of the sword. Then, Adam whipped her cheek with the tip of the silver chain. The touch was light, and yet the sizzle was discernible even to Margaret's ears, and when the demon cried out in pain, grasping the wound with a hand filthy and gnarled, Adam struck the killing blow. The sword slid into her chest and out again, her body barely resisting the force of Adam's arm, and she fell to the ground as though she were a mere mortal.

There was no blood around the blade, and no fluid leaked from the puncture site. She must not have fed recently. Where had she been when the frenzy had overtaken her brothers and sisters?

Adam drove the blade into the body again, and again, to be sure he'd hit his mark. He grunted with the effort of shearing through bone as hard as rock. When it was apparent he had finished his work, his sword lowered, his chest heaving and his breath coming in hard huffs, Margaret cautiously approached, not wishing to startle him.

"She needs to burn," Adam said, not quite a question, but seeking confirmation all the same.

Margaret nodded distractedly as she looked down at the dead demon. Dirty and lean, clothed in rags, and slack of face, the vampire was almost pitiful. Her beauty was still apparent in the lines of her cheekbones and nose and brow, but the glamour of it was gone.

Adam nodded. "I'll fetch tinder and return with a flame," he said before leaving the room through the broken wall.

Margaret's mind wandered as she stared at the body until her eyes looked through it completely and she lost herself in her thoughts. There were things she needed to say to Adam when he returned, but she didn't like to admit it. She was not a woman who required favors of others.

He was by her side again within minutes. He dragged the body to the open courtyard and set it beside a stack of brush he'd set to burning. It seemed to resist the heat, so he added a little more fuel and pushed the body closer to the flames.

Shockingly, the blaze suddenly took, and the body yielded to the fire. Margaret turned her face away from the uncomfortable warmth, raising her arms instinctively and stepping away to escape the stifling air. When the burning subsided a little, she looked back to see a small pile of smoldering ashes where the corpse had been.

"You will need to locate a receptacle to collect the ashes," Margaret directed. "I'll transfer them to silver when we return to the village."

Adam saw to the task with efficiency. Before long, they were standing in the still darkness, preparing for a long journey on foot through the trees and under the moon.

"I...I must tell you," Adam stammered, his eyes on the ground. "It was...harder...to fight this she-demon than it was to execute those monsters in the village today." His hunched shoulders spoke of shame, not relief, at his revelation. "I feared for a moment that both our lives were forfeit tonight."

Margaret fought back a great wave of fear. If Adam's magic was fading, all was lost, yet she could not—would not—believe it was possible.

"Ye did very well," she praised him gruffly. "And I do not think the Master's curse will be so easily ended. His magic is not to be taken so lightly. Mayhap there is more to learn."

"Aye," he said with a shrug closer to a roll of his shoulders, and Margaret sensed her words had heartened him.

"This is not how I had planned for our journey to end," she went on vaguely. "I was meant to slay the devil here, but the devil was gone."

Adam looked around the open yard, his eyes pausing near the altar. Margaret suspected the patch of ground that held his attention was where they'd abandoned the body.

"I offer you my apologies, and our only defense that we knew no better."

Carefully now, she said, "My fear is that the Master will seek to reclaim his magic, either himself or by the incubus in the dream, or by sending his creatures to do his bidding on Earth. I am well able to protect myself in the aether, but as for the other…." She feigned distracted thought, to allow time for Adam to draw his own conclusions.

"I can protect you," he declared earnestly, and Margaret breathed deeply in relief. She had correctly judged his sense of obligation.

"You would embrace the power the Master of Fear has bestowed upon you?" she asked quietly.

Adam frowned. "I would if I could use it to destroy his children and defeat his rule on Earth." His eyes glowed in the rising moonlight. "I would like nothing more than to use his own magic against him."

Margaret bit her lip against the smile that threatened to undo her manipulations.

"And the others? Will they see things this way?"

"I will make sure of it."

Margaret made a show of straightening her clothes, taking care not to appear too eager to accept his proposal. Let no one believe they have granted a favor. She disliked owing anybody anything.

"But in return for our service, witch, I would ask

something of you."

Margaret looked at the big man with narrowed eyes, berating herself for having underestimated his intelligence. Her hostility was genuine this time. "And what would that be?"

"We are alone and…frightened. We came to you, seeking cure and counsel, and we will have that from you, one way or another. Will you agree to an exchange of service? Our eternal protection on Earth for your continued instruction and…comfort."

Margaret stared long enough for Adam to shuffle his feet, but he did not break away from her gaze. She knew how much strength that took. Her ice-blue eyes were unpleasant to meet for long.

"Very well," she said with a show of reluctance she did not entirely feel. If she had to have protectors for The Fates knew how long, it was better they be required to follow her word. This wasn't a joining of equals. She was their guide, and that was a happy outcome she had not anticipated but would gladly accept.

Adam let out a breath, and Margaret's heart went out to him, just a little. She wasn't made of stone, as was a demon. Perhaps now she could afford to be a little more generous with this man who had promised to stand between her and death.

"Adam, here is my first piece of advice." He looked at her with eyes so hungry for hope that she really did soften this time. She reached out a hand, and he took it. His skin was warm, and Margaret pressed it gently. "The Master's magic has made you humanity's greatest asset. You're not only my defenders but defenders of all. Vampire slayers, they shall call you, with the strength and the speed and the senses of the vampire, but without his sinful nature. The people will rejoice, Adam, for now, we have true hope, where before there were only empty wishes and unanswered prayers."

It appeared at first Adam would rebuff her attempt to improve his spirits, but then the words struck home, and emotion washed over his face. He stood taller and gripped the hilt of his sword, looking almost regal.

"Let us go," he said. "I would return to my brothers, and then to my wife, and tomorrow…With the rise of the sun dawns a new world, and we must be ready."

Margaret held on tight to the magic. "A new world," she agreed grimly.

Adam nodded at the precious bundle in her grip. "What do ye intend to do with that?"

"I plan to hide it in a place where nobody can find it," she whispered, realizing that prayers still had a place in this strange new world, and she offered one up right then and there.

She was a dreamer, after all, and nowhere was safer for her, or the devil's magic, than in that world beyond sleep.

Lord, let that be true.

ACKNOWLEDGMENTS

The *Magic of the Vampire* saga has been such fun to write. Escaping into the world of Seth Callaghan (and Riley Quinn and Finn O'Brien) is, for me, an exercise in chasing joy, pure and simple. I'm only glad I have so much more of their tale to tell, and so many more reasons to lose myself in the magic and the romance of these special people.

And on the subject of special people, there are many I need to thank for their ongoing support, enthusiasm, and contributions to helping me take *pure / evil* from inception to print: Shay Laurent, Maria Spada, Michelle Rascon, Alain Davis and Lisa Henson. And a shout-out to my incredible online writing community, a found family of generous word wizards who are only too happy to share their wisdom when it's needed most.

AVAILABLE NOW!
MAGIC OF THE VAMPIRE: BOOK ONE

love luck

"Close your eyes," he murmured, and my lids snapped shut. He picked up my hand and ran the tip of his icy nose along the inside of my forearm, from the pulse at my wrist to the crease at my elbow ... His lips brushed mine as he whispered wordlessly, bewitchingly, then the scent of his skin overwhelmed my senses, and the world lost its foundations beneath me.

Riley Quinn loves her quirky great-grandmother, but her superstitions are seriously irritating. Grams may believe in lucky silver jewelry and beautiful demons who hunt humans in the night, but Riley knows it's all nonsense.

Until Seth Callaghan arrives in town.

Riley's best friend, sexy surfer Finn O'Brien, begs her to ignore the new guy. Grams demands she stay away. Yet Riley is magnetically drawn to the sweet seduction of Seth's charms.

But all is not what it seems. Soon, Riley finds herself swept up in a supernatural world beyond her understanding.

Secrets and lies.

Magic and power.

Vampires and temptation.

Life...and death.

As danger swirls around her, Riley's loved ones fight to protect her from the darkness closing in—but only Riley can decide her fate. Torn between love and lust, loyalty and destiny, Riley's survival isn't guaranteed when she's hunted by the devil himself.

COMING SOON!
MAGIC OF THE VAMPIRE:
PREQUEL NOVELLA

WANT / NEED

Seth Callaghan is a reluctant incubus, cursed with the power to seduce
and satisfy his willing victims—all in exchange for their souls.

It's a hateful magic, and he refuses to indulge.
The price is too high to pay…again.

When he's called to fulfill a centuries-old duty to protect a girl
with the power to save the world, Seth has no idea she will demolish
the walls he's painfully built around his dead, broken heart.

Drawn like a moth to a flame, Seth wants this young witch more
than he's ever wanted anyone, but she alone holds the key
to destroying him completely.

Blood and lust.

Dreams and fire.

Survival and sacrifice.

Desire…and death.

Riley Quinn is Seth Callaghan's doom, and he needs to stay away.
But want and need are two very different things.

Printed in Great Britain
by Amazon